MY FIRST BEST FRIEND

STILL A DREAM.

SAINATH ROHIT

So many Memories, and so many stunts, happened in school life. Friendship, Love, Feelings, Emotions, Bonds, Vibes etc.

Have you ever thought, that my love / crush started at age of 8. Feeling of crush, at that age is so kidding.

This is school life. As we make new friends. Learn new things and build our career there. It is the only time which,

We enjoy most, and when we enter college, we always miss our school life. School life teaches us lots of new things and prepares us to face all the challenges of life.

Among all the students, some students have a different view regarding of the teachers, the strict attitude of parents, the compulsions for completing homework and the regular attendance in schools are some of the unhappy aspects of this period. They do not feel free in their schools and wish to be like the birds that fly free.

The students do not like strict discipline that has to be followed while studying in a school.

But, My school life was different. My school was including all the above rules with extra masala.

We still miss our school day, But not to every student have the same feeling, which I have.

.

My First day of the school, I got new friends. New environment, new faces, and I was afraid. I was siting in the
last bench of middle row. My First class teacher name was Vijay

Lakshmi Teacher. Class started, all the students were getting introduced.

Then, I heard his name, "Abhiroop". I just wondered what type of name it is !!?.

His name was different from others. I thought that "Abhiroop" meaning is that, he will change his roop (shape) depending on the behavior of the students. haha I used to think like that.

But I was wrong, day by day he was good to others and me too...don't know why, he looks special for me. One day we sat together, and he was normal with me. I don't know what to talk. I said to myself that...(arey yaar he is not a girl)

Slowly we became close, and we started knowing about each other very well. I was being true with him, and he too was being the same with me. Not only that, but I was happy that I got a friend who could bear all my happiness and sadness. Furthermore, I requested god that, not to break our friendship."Since" first class he was my best friend.

We will sit together, eat together, go play together and many more. I was happy with my friendship and suddenly one atom bomb was blast in our 3rd class.

Sameera, she was very cute and very sweet. Obviously Children will be loyal and sweet to their friends.

All the class hate her because she will be not close to anyone.

She wants to sit alone and study.

She was family wali bachhi ! Having crush in school days was Awesome feeling in the life.

And that too in 3rd class...LOL. ! I was having a crush on her.

I said to abhiroop that I like her. On the cultural event day we all became friends.

All were dancing and playing together.

There was a big smile on our face, all were meeting each other and making friends.We all were happy at that moment.

In the next day, all are present, expect sameera. I was disappointed that she is absent but unfortunately she came to school. She was late.

Finally, she sat behind me. Abhiroop sat beside me, obviously best friends will have so much stuff to talk, and we will make fun of each other and laugh like an idiot.

If we get scoldings from our teacher or sir, automatically smile comes to our face.

We can't control it. And the day has come, finally sameera sawed me and talked to me regarding subject related doubt. I was managing that

I know everything. But My idiot abhiroop was laughing.

And she also started laughing at me.

I was like oh god!. I scolded him a lot after the school.

He was like, ok I will make you both move closer. I was like, ok done.

And next day she started sitting behind us....as usually we will do jokes, and slowly she turned back and started laughing. From that day i and abhiroop and cracking jokes in every period.

In class, if I was punished, abhi will crack jokes on me and I will laugh on him in front of all.

If he was punished, I will crack a joke on him in front of all and my main focus will be on sameera that, she is enjoying my jokes or else she is feeling annoying.

I got to know from her smile that she was enjoying my jokes. I was happy with my best friend Abhiroop and my favorite person sameera.

Day by day she was becoming close to me and my jokes. She said, she is happy to have me and abhiroop in her life. We 3 became good friend in 3rd class.
One fine day in front of all she clenched my chicks and said you are so cute and chubby. I was shocked! I was blushing by lying on the bench.

And the same she said to abhiroop. And she also said that, she likes him.
I was like hew....ok......my mind was blank.

I didn't understand anything. She was looking at abhiroop and smiling, and he was doing showoff in front of her by saying, ho.... Really !?.

I suddenly stood up, and I said I will come in few minutes. I went to restroom, and my tears are unstoppable. Furthermore, I was blank. Not only that, but I thought, if she like abhiroop it's not his fault. Likewise, I have to change my mindset and be positive on them.

On that day I was not cracking jokes on abhiroop, and I was not close to sameera also.

Sameera have been trying to talk to me every day.

But I was just avoiding her like nibba nibbi love story.
Abhiroop got to know the reason behind my silence. He was not sorry to me. I was like it's ok.
Suddenly we got barriers in between us for few days. I was ok with sameera and abhiroop. I said to them, I
don't have any bad intention on you both.

They were clear that, they are not in love. But I'm not that type of person which, I can't handle the vibe and
closeness between them. They were ok with me. But I was not ok with them. I can't see my best friend loving
my crush.

But in the matter of friendship, I was ready to sacrifice her, And I did. But unfortunately she took TC in 4th
class, and she took admission in another school. Abhiroop was in a

shock by listening that she is no more in
our school. And I was totally broken. I cried a lot for her.

But we didn't try to get her address, contact number and her school name nothing we knew about her. We are not CID officers to investigate about her and drag the details...! Come on yaar we are in 4th class only. We don't even got the thought to take her number. But that was a Good feelings in my school life.
I don't know where is sameera, how she is and what she is doing.

I just knew that her name is sameera, she has curly hairs, and she is cute and sweet. Still now I remember her face. I ask the same question to abhiroop in 2019. He was like, who is she??.

So coming to 4th class. Our class teacher was Usha rani teacher. We were growing up day by day. I have learned new bad words from abhiroop, and I was applying to my all friends. I was very happy to apply them the bad words.

I was enjoying by scolding others. At one day i and abhi were sitting at last bench.
We were having hind period. We were so naughty in the class. Furthermore, we are cracking many jokes and laughing like a hell. We have a habit to lift the bench from below with the foot.

Furthermore, we were lifting and also we were scared of falling down, Our aim is to lift the bench up, and we have to get tense of falling down, and we have to laugh. That's it !

We are in last bench, and we had a gap between wall and last bench. We do not have a support to make balance at our back. Finally, it was my turn, I lifted the bench more than the limit, and we have fallen down in slow motion. We're hiding our faces with hands stick to the floor and our Hindi madam came to us. She was like "Ayyooo are you ok beta".

She was pampering us, and she was checking us that we are good or crying. But, we idiots were laughing non-stop. We are in a hurry to cover our laughing face in front of our teacher. This was the memorable and unforgettable day in my life.

I still remember it and I laugh the same as I used to laugh before. Few days before, abhiroop said about his plan. That, he was leaving with his family to his relatives house.

Which is out of station. I started crying, I was begging him please don't go. But he was helpless. I was not in a good mood the whole day.

I can't even imagine a day without him in the class. And I know I can't be far from him. His presence is oxygen for me. But he was

about to go next day. I made myself strong, and I was like please come soon. I will be waiting for you. He felt emotional about me. He, too, got tears. But he
controlled.

All my friends were saying why are you crying like a girl, he will come back. Chill yaar....etc they were
saying to me.

But I know what he is for me and what I feel about him without his presence. He was the only
best friend for me since 3 and 1/2 years. I can't even leave him like that.
Finally, he went.

From the day he went I was like "Nobitha waiting for his doraemon". Finally, he was back
after 1 week. The day he came I gave him a tight hug and kiss on his chicks. All were like chiii chiiii. I was like
haha. Again my doors of Happiness were open by abhi, coming back to class.

Days passed on and one fine day I was not happy. This class was a hell to me all the Sections
changed. Abhiroop is no more in my class. I was in 'A' section, and he was in 'B'.

I just had a point in my mind
that, sameera left, it's ok I have abhiroop in my life, I was like no need

to worry. I will be happy and make him
happy this year too. But we got a long distance between us.

I got new friends, he also got new friends and I swear no one was like abhiroop. I was missing him from 2 to
3 weeks. He was normal, no missing and nothing. We will meet only in lunchtime and break time. That to
only for few minutes. I was missing my true friend.

Now we are in 6th class again new friends and girls. Again distractions and masthi. I was doing all my masthi
and enjoying all my days with new friends with Abhi.

I was feeling very bad, and he was also not willing to
meet me as we used to meet before. Again we gather together in 9th class. He was still my best friend. Again
we sat together and all the fun and masthi repeat. And again girls, distraction etc. We have got more new
friends in 9th class.

I accept I look ugly in my past. But, I'm good now. I'm beside abhiroop. Abhiroop is in dark blue color t-shirt.

We were called as Junior 10th class. Again I got wounded with new friends, Rohit singh, sumit singh, ashish,
Ashwin, Jai Kumar, sai mahesh, saleem mallik, janghir mallik, Ruthvik kumar, dhanush, niharika.K, niharika. B, Deepika kothari, manav sharma, bhavya reddy goutam, pranay yadav, shanmukha, hrithik kumar, Shaik Ibhrahim, manish, krishna agarwal, krishna kanth heda, Rajeeth chetty, dhanraj, Nitesh raj (class topper),
pavan kumar etc.

Abhiroop is in dark blue color t-shirt and this is my 10th class batch.

This is on Republic day. @mamatha madam.

All colorful friends with colorful world. It was a new feeling to me. But I have never replaced Abhiroop among these.

This day was our Farewell party.Joash, Ashish, Dhanush, And I.It was organized in Swagath Grand Hotel_Himayat Nagar.

He is special for me and will be special for me throughout my life. We have done with our 10th
class.

So many feelings, emotions, and happiness we left behind. Ahiroop and all my friends left. I was so depressed about leaving all. That's too all of a sudden. But it's life we have to move on.

For every friendship day I used to go to abhiroop house and give him gifts. His mom n dad were so nice towards me, and they too knew that I was his best-best-bestttt friend for his life. I had invited Abhiroop and Joash to my house.

Abhiroop and Joash (October_2014).

But I was wrong about him. When I was in Degree I and my friend alpha went to abhiroop house to celebrate his birthday. He came out with long hairs and thick Beard.

He was looking handsome. I was very happy to see him after long time. I have contacted him so many times. But he was not in Hyderabad. He went out of station with his cousins.

And finally met him on his birthday in degree. He was studying b.tech and also he started his career in sports.
I was so happy for him. I and my Alpha made his birthday so special and awesome we were again laughing like our school days.

I, Alpha, And Abhiroop (March_2019)

That was the bond between me and abhiroop. Alpha was also my best friend, and he
knew everything about abhiroop. We were laughing on the streets like mad people.

One we bond together Na
we will not care anyone. We will have our own vibe of masthi and laundpana !

I have never been lied to abhi, and I have shared all my secrets to him.....he is one of my loved person.
You can know my value of friendship one you see both of us together.

After his birthday in 2019 we never met him again. In my life lots of things happened, and I was very eagerly
waiting to tell all my stuff to abhiroop. I share with him everything including my personal life. But, after his
birthday.

I have contacted him 100 times 500 messages and went to his home many times. I have got to
know that he got hired in photography job. He is very passionate about capturing images. He also has a tattoo on his right hand. It looks Awesome.

Enter Caption

I got to knew it by his Instagram post. I have dropped a comment on his post and tried to DM him....then also
no use. Now we are in 2022 till now I'm trying to contact him.

I will go near his house and stand in front of his house. I will stare at his door.... Furthermore, I have a hope that he will definitely come outside. But that hope is still a dream for me. I have no guts to go to his house directly.

Because there is no response from the person for 3 years. I'm still waiting for his reply and call. Because, I don't want to miss a friend like Abhi.

May be, he may be busy......but I'm still waiting for his friendship to come back and be as like we used to be before.

I have to tell him many miracles which I have passed these many years. I'm not angry on him, or I don't have any revenge on him.

I just want to make my friendship live. And with Ego and Attitude I don't want to lose his friendship. Because, it's hard to find a friend like my ABHI.

Finally, missing him a lot..... In life special people come only once, once you miss them, they're never going to come back.!

Be in their presence when ever they are with you or in front of you. Please pause your ego and attitude in front of Loved once. They are the only person who likes you as how you are now !

They're not going to
change your life, not going to judge you, they're not going to show
your attitude if they are true Friends.

See the life in perspective way, if Parents are our Road, Bridge is our
friends, if traffic signal are our Exams,
traffic police are our Lecturers. All will show us the Right way, but
when and where to stop and where to
escape is depend upon you.

If you go through from all situation, you will get to know what are the
difficulties
you must face in the future, and it will be easy for you.

But, if you take shortcut from the lane, you don't what is going to be
the future, and you will face many difficulties.

Think once !

Miss you my dear friend, in future I want to enjoy my success with you
if I fail I want to share my pain with
you......whatever the matter may be. But in my life you are Mandatory !

STILL WAITING FOR YOUR REPLY...
Yours Lovingly Sainath Rohit.

Contents

Printed by Libri Plureos GmbH in Hamburg,
Germany